This book is for my son John, who first taught me
Lala salama— the Swahili words meaning "Sleep peacefully."
And for Karen and Ella Nuru, who I'm sure hear those words from him, too.
With love, P. M.

To Mom, Daddy, and Denny
E. Z.

Text copyright © 2011 by Patricia MacLachlan
Illustrations copyright © 2011 by Elizabeth Zunon

First edition 2011

Library of Congress Cataloging-in-Publication Data

MacLachlan, Patricia.
Lala salama : a Tanzanian lullaby / Patricia MacLachlan ; illustrated by Elizabeth Zunon. — 1st ed.
p. cm.
Summary: A mother relates the events of a peaceful day along the banks of
Lake Tanganyika to her baby, wrapped up and ready for sleep.

ISBN 978-0-7636-4747-6

[1. Mother and child — Fiction. 2. Family life — Tanzania — Fiction.
3. Tanganyika, Lake — Fiction. 4. Tanzania — Fiction.] I. Zunon, Elizabeth, ill. II. Title.
PZ7.M2225Lal 2011
[E] — dc22   2010040465

11 12 13 14 15 16 SCP 10 9 8 7 6 5 4 3 2 1

Printed in Humen, Dongguan, China

This book was typeset in Old Claude.
The illustrations were done in oil paint on watercolor paper.

Candlewick Press
99 Dover Street
Somerville, Massachusetts 02144

visit us at www.candlewick.com

Lala Salama

A Tanzanian Lullaby

Patricia MacLachlan

illustrated by Elizabeth Zunon

CANDLEWICK PRESS

LONG AGO, this morning,
the sun rose
above the hill
above our house,
spilling light over the hills of the Congo
and the lake with the beautiful name,
Tanganyika,
like a song.

Lala salama, little one.

You watched your *baba*
brush his carved wooden boat clean
and sweep out dust and twigs
and the leavings of birds.
Out on the lake were other boats,
their flour-sack sails
fat with wind.

I washed your face and hands
in the water warmed by the fire
and poured water over your feet.
I dressed you in white
and wrapped you in a long colorful *kanga*.

I filled the water jug,
you on my back,

and worked the fields,
you on my back,

and cooked the food,
   you on my back —
close enough to feel the beating of your heart.

Lala salama. Hush.

Now the monkeys swing from
branch to branch,
going to their treetop beds.
The shy zebra mama comes with her baby
to drink fresh water.

The bee-eaters twitter their last songs of the day
before the sun falls down
over the faraway hills,
leaving a rose red world behind.

Lala salama.

We take Baba a basket of food
and a lantern for the night.
Baba hugs and kisses you —
both of you smiling,
both of you laughing.
Your *baba* sings his own sweet song
in his own sweet voice.

Lala salama. Dream your dreams.

I lift you out of the *kanga*.
You and I sit by the gentle fire
next to our home with the golden thatched roof,
watching the tall clouds,
watching the night come.

The stars spread across the sky.
One by one by one, the lanterns
flicker on the lake —
    stars above and stars below.
You and I know that
one of those lights is Baba's light.

The fire glows.
Close your eyes,
my
dear
child.

Lala salama.